Pumpkin Time

For Jennifer,
whose story it is.

J.A.

For Louise,
Roy and Mark.

K.L.

Canadian Cataloguing in Publication Data

Andrews, Jan, 1942-
    Pumpkin time

ISBN 0-88899-112-6

I. LaFave, Kim. II. Title.

PS8551.N46P85 1990   jC813'.54   C90-093594-4
PZ7.A52Pu 1990

A Groundwood Book
Douglas & McIntyre Ltd.
585 Bloor Street West
Toronto, Canada M6G 1K5

Design by Michael Solomon
Printed and bound in Hong Kong
by Everbest Printing Co. Ltd.

PUMPKIN TIME

BY Jan Andrews
PICTURES BY Kim LaFave

A Groundwood Book
Douglas & McIntyre
Toronto/Vancouver

THEY were afraid at first — coming downstairs in the morning to find a pumpkin in the kitchen where their mother should have been.

They stood together, huddled in the doorway. "She was always saying she'd turn into one," Danya whispered.

"Whenever she had to work late," Sean agreed.

He took a step towards the great round shape, then hesitated. "You are sure it's her, aren't you?"

Rachel nodded. "She's still got her scarf on. And there's her tea, on the table by her earrings."

"What'll we do?" Tears were starting to fill Sean's eyes.

"We'll have to look after her," Rachel said.

"How, Rach?" Danya asked.

"Going to school and to after-school — like we always do — so no one will ask any questions. I mean, if anyone found out, they'd want to take her away. They'd want to take care of us or something."

"There's her work, though."
"We'll phone in like she does.
We'll say she's lost her voice
and can't come to the phone."

Sean touched the pumpkin
very gently. "If we go to school,
she'll be all by herself."

Danya picked up Mum's mug and
held it. "Mum's always all right," she said.

All day at school they hoped Mum would
change back to her old self again.

"Do you think we should tell Dad?" Danya asked when they were back home. Rachel shook her head.

She went to the fridge and got out food for supper. They ate toasted ketchup sandwiches and hot dogs, with pickles.

Taking his plate, Sean sat as close to the pumpkin as he could. "If she's going to stay a pumpkin, do you think she ought to be outside with the other pumpkins in the garden?"

"She's our mother. Slugs would slime on her."

"Anyway, she's happy," Rachel protested. "You can see it. She's putting out leaves."

By morning there were more leaves. "There's a sound, too," Danya noticed. "Like a song."

"Pumpkinny, but..."

"Sort of Mum-ish."

The pumpkin leaves shook and waved a little. Suddenly, Sean grinned.

After breakfast, they set off to school again. It was their weekend with their dad, so they didn't come back home till Sunday evening.

They headed straight for the kitchen. The plant had spread and increased itself. It had become a huge, amazing, springing, flowering vine. One whole corner of the room was filled with it. It reached along the ceiling, climbing and twining up and over.

"She's made a cave almost," Sean murmured.

"Let's get mattresses from the basement."

"Let's bring blankets and pillows."

They snuggled down to sleep together, the leaves and tendrils of the pumpkin nestling against them, folding round them closer.

"She won't grow over us, will she?" Rachel whispered.

"She's our mother," Danya said. Then, sleepily, "The song's bigger, too."

"It isn't louder."

"Just sort of more."

There were new flowers on the vine in the morning — bright clear yellow ones. The kitchen had an earthy, comfy fragrance. Rachel breathed longingly, got up and then lay down again. "It's a P.D. day." The pumpkin stirred through every leaf stalk.

"She's all pleased. Usually on P.D. days she's all worried."

Sean reached for the cornflakes. "Don't you think she'll be getting hungry?"

"We can't put compost on her!"

"But she hasn't had anything to eat for days."

"We'll read her a story," Rachel said.

The pumpkin leaves seemed to stretch and open even further, brushing the children's hands, touching their cheeks a little.

"What kind of a story?"

"Like she read us when we were little." The flowers danced and grew brighter.

"I know. Her favourite." Sean went to the bookshelf. "The one about the bay and the sea and the summer." The song filled all the kitchen.

"It's a good one to start with," Rachel said.

They finished the book and chose another. About noon, they heard rain against the windows. They brought paints and plasticine and made models and pictures. They talked, remembering things they had done together, and sometimes they just sat.

Night fell again. Before they slept, they sipped hot chocolate and ate apple sandwiches.

"I wish we didn't have to go to school tomorrow," Sean said.

"We can come back, though. She'll be here every single evening."

Danya let one of the pumpkin's tendrils curl round her finger. "I don't remember her so peaceful, ever. Do you think she just got tired? I mean, with work and us and everything?"

"Maybe. Yes."

It was a wonderful week. Never before had there been one like it.

There was food in the fridge to last for ages. They didn't have to worry.

But by Friday they found themselves
coming home more slowly.

"It was different before," Danya said as they stood in the hallway hanging up their coats. "The house was all full of rushing about and being busy."

"It was Mum's busyness. You'd come in, and the busyness would be there when she wasn't even home yet."

"When she got in she'd make jokes and stuff."

"Or get mad at us — like when we didn't put our boots away."

Tears pricked at Sean's eyes. "I miss it, how it used to be."

In the kitchen, the pumpkin leaves drooped a little. It was only round the edges. Still, they couldn't help but notice.

"We've hurt her feelings," Rachel insisted.

Danya touched the pumpkin stem near the base where it was rough and sharp and bristly, shaking her head. "In the night," she said, "I woke up. The song wasn't the same anymore."

"I'm going upstairs," Sean muttered.

They sat on
Mum's bed in her
bedroom. "What if
she wants to get back
and she doesn't know how?"

"We should help her. She's
our mother."

"We should let her out or something."

Danya ran off downstairs. Rachel and Sean followed. Danya picked up Mum's mug. She cupped her hands around it firmly. "What I think is — Mum will manage. Mum will know what to do," she said.

That night they made a feast for themselves — baked beans and sausages, and canned ravioli. They read more stories. It was late before they drifted into sleep.

They had no idea how the window came open...

They only knew they woke in the morning; their faces very cold. There were leaves on the floor and flowers all withered. Their mother was beside them.

"It's freezing," she grumbled. "What on earth do you guys think you're up to?"

Rachel and Sean got up to close the window.

"Hi, Mum," Danya said.